MATTHEW AND THE
MIDNIGHT MOVIE

Published in Canada in 2002 by Stoddart Kids,
a division of Stoddart Publishing Co. Limited
895 Don Mills Road, 400–2 Park Centre, Toronto, Ontario M3C 1W3

Published in the United States in 2002 by Stoddart Kids
a division of Stoddart Publishing Co. Limited
PMB 128, 4500 Witmer Estates, Niagara Falls, New York 14305-1386

www.stoddartkids.com

To order Stoddart Kids books please contact General Distribution Services
In Canada Tel. (416) 213-1919 FAX (416) 213-1917
Email cservice@genpub.com
In the United States Toll-free tel. 1-800-805-1083 Toll-free FAX 1-800-481-6207
Email gdsinc@genpub.com

06 05 04 03 02   1 2 3 4 5

Canadian Cataloguing in Publication Data

Morgan, Allen, 1946–
Matthew and the midnight movie

ISBN 0-7737-6273-6

I. Martchenko, Michael II. Title.

PS8576.O642M273 2002   jC813'.54   C2001-902925-X
PZ7.M8203Matm 2002

*Matthew, star of his own action/adventure movie, rescues his mother, foils the
Incredible Invisible Shrinking Man, and wins a Harry Award, all before sunrise.*

THE CANADA COUNCIL | LE CONSEIL DES ARTS
FOR THE ARTS | DU CANADA
SINCE 1957 | DEPUIS 1957

*We acknowledge for their financial support of our
publishing program the Canada Council, the Ontario Arts
Council, and the Government of Canada through the
Book Publishing Industry Development Program (BPIDP).*

*Printed and bound in Hong Kong, China
Book Art Inc., Toronto*

MATTHEW AND THE
MIDNIGHT
MOVIE

by Allen Morgan
Illustrated by Michael Martchenko

Stoddart
Kids
TORONTO • NEW YORK

One rainy Saturday afternoon, Matthew rented a movie called *Raiders of the Lost Ark*.

"Hero stuff isn't hard to do," he told his mother when it was through. "I could rescue you, no problem at all, if I had a good hat."

His mother agreed. She poked around the closet and found one for him to wear. When Matthew tried it on, he looked exactly like Indiana Jones — only different.

"Now we can make a movie, too," Matthew told her. "We'll even get some real stars like the Incredible Invisible Shrinking Man."

"Is he the bad guy?" his mother asked.

"He's *very* bad," Matthew said. "I'll have to put on a special disguise and chase him around. Don't worry, Mom, your part is easy. Just act surprised whenever things happen."

Matthew went down to the basement to get the movie set ready. He opened the lid of the washing machine and put in a coil of rope. He left the knot at the end sticking out, and it looked very much like the head of a snake if you didn't look twice, which you probably wouldn't.

A few minutes later, Matthew's mother came down to do the laundry. When she saw the snake she was somewhat confused. But when Matthew dumped the dirty laundry onto her head, she was truly amazed. She stared at Matthew in disbelief as he wrestled the Incredible Invisible Shrinking Man.

"What's going on?" she asked.

"It's the movie, Mom! It's me!" he said, as he took off his disguise. "You did just great. You looked very surprised, and this was just the rehearsal. Everything will be even better when we shoot the movie. We'll have real spiders instead of the laundry and hire a poisonous cobra snake. We can use the rope, then, to tie you up. I'll get you a blindfold, too!"

Later that night when it was time for bed, Matthew was feeling a little bit worried about his mother.

"What if a bad guy actually came? What would you do?" He gave her his bicycle bell to ring in case she was part of a kidnapping. "Ring for me. You don't need Indiana Jones," he told her.

"Of course not, dear. I'm sure you would do a much better rescue."

"Well, I would," Matthew said. "When we make the movie, you'll see."

His mother smiled and turned out the light. She tucked him in and kissed him goodnight. As Matthew lay awake in the dark, he thought he heard a bell outside ringing softly in the night. He didn't see how it could be his mother, since she was still in the house, but before he could really tell for sure, he fell fast asleep.

Around about midnight Matthew woke up. The sound of the bell was louder now, so he went to the window. A menacing figure was tying up a man. He laughed aloud as he tightened the knots. Then he lit a big stick of dynamite and left the scene. Matthew put on his hero hat and ran outside.

A streetcar full of midnight turkeys came clanging wildly down the track. The music swelled as "The Trolley Song" blared from hidden speakers. Matthew rescued the man just in time. They got away a few seconds before the dynamite blew.

There was a dramatic pause as the feathers settled. Then all of a sudden the director appeared. "Cut!" he shouted.

"Welcome to the movies, kid," the man Matthew had rescued said. "I'm known to my fans as Illinois Smith. What handle do you go by, boy?"

"Matthew Holmes."

"Kid, you need a movie name. You're from Canada, right? I can tell by the hat. I went to Winnipeg once on a wager, so why don't we call you Manitoba Matt?"

"Actually, I'm from Ontario," Matthew explained.

"Kid, it doesn't matter, it's just a movie! I'm from New Jersey, originally. You and me, we could be the North American Terrific Twosome. We'd be just the team to finally catch the Incredible Invisible Shrinking Man."

"I've heard about him," Matthew replied. "Is he in our movie, too?"

"Sure he is, kid. There he is now, up on your roof, and he's kidnapping someone. Who is that lady, anyway?"

A bicycle bell rang out in the night, and Matthew knew who she was all right. "That's no lady," Matthew cried, "that's my mother!"

When the director saw what was happening, he called for the crew to turn on the lights. "Action!" he shouted. The Incredible Invisible Shrinking Man slung Matthew's mother up over his shoulder and jumped onto the roof of a passing streetcar. For a moment it looked like he might escape, but luckily another streetcar was coming down the tracks. Illinois Smith grabbed Matthew's arm and they leapt on board.

"Follow that streetcar!" he shouted to the driver.

"Usually do," the driver replied.

Matthew's streetcar was very fast, but just before it finally caught up, the Incredible Invisible Shrinking Man jumped down to the street with Matthew's mother and disappeared through the door of a nearby department store.

The Terrific Twosome followed close behind. When they got inside the store, they decided to use some special disguises to keep things confusing. The plan worked well. The Incredible Invisible Shrinking Man couldn't tell they were there at all. When he finally stopped to take a rest in the toy department, Matthew leapt out of hiding.

"Unhand my mother!" he cried.

The Incredible Invisible Shrinking Man was cornered all right, but he still had a trick or two left. He took out a sprayer and squirted himself, *Squoooosh*! He shrunk himself down to tiny size and he shrunk Matthew's mother too! He threw her into a racing car and laughed as he drove away.

The sprayer was left behind, so Matthew grabbed it and sprayed himself. Illinois Smith did the same. When they were shrunk, they jumped into a toy RV and the chase was on!

They tore through the store from end to end, past hardware and software and underwear. They zoomed through living rooms, kitchens, and dens. They came close to crashing in women's fashions, but soon they went racing off again.

The chase finally ended in the bedroom display. The Incredible Invisible Shrinking Man grabbed Matthew's mother, and ran from the car. He didn't get far. The shrinking spray was wearing off, and he had to stop while he grew. The Terrific Twosome were growing, too. They rolled down their windows and jumped just in time. A moment later they were regular size.

"I'm taking you in," Matthew told his foe.

The Incredible Invisible Shrinking Man didn't seem worried. He took off his hat and undid his coat. He kicked off his boots, one by one.

"He's disappearing!" moaned Illinois Smith. "We'll never catch him now!"

Matthew knew that he had to do something. He grabbed a spread from a nearby bed and threw it over the villain's head.

"You think fast, kid," said Illinois Smith, as he snapped the handcuffs in place.

Matthew climbed up onto the bed to see if his mother was OK. For a moment or two it was hard to say, but then she snored. He removed the tape and untied the ropes. When he tucked her in with a goodnight kiss, her eyelids fluttered open.

"You look familiar," she told Matthew. "Who are you, anyway?"

"I better not say," Matthew replied. "I'm in disguise."

"Your moustache kind of tickles," she said, and drifted back to sleep.

"That's a wrap!" the director shouted. "You're aces, kid. Best performance I've seen in years." The crew all clapped and some of them cheered.

"I bet you even get an award," said Illinois Smith. "They call them the Harrys and they're giving them out at the banquet tonight. Come on, let's go!"

"What about my mother?" asked Matthew. "I can't just leave her here."

"She'll be OK," said the director. "We'll take her home in the limo."

So Matthew went to the awards banquet. He was glad that he did. He won a Harry for the "Best New Face in a Rescue Race".

"I want to thank my mom for this," he told the cheering crowd. "If she hadn't been there for me tonight, there would never have been a rescue!"

When the Harry Awards were finally over, Illinois Smith drove Matthew home.

"I wish my mom had been able to see the way I made the movie tonight," Matthew sighed.

"She saw it, kid," said Illinois Smith. "The movie we made was broadcast live to the Dreaming Channel. Whoever was sleeping could tune right in." He dropped Matthew off and waved goodnight.

Matthew waved back and went up to his room. Soon he was fast asleep.

Matthew woke up at half past five. He ran into his mother's room to see if she'd made it back home. She had. His bicycle bell was by the bed, so he rang it over her head once or twice to let her know he was there.

"What's that?" she groaned, as she opened her eyes.

"The rescue bell," Matthew replied. "You used it last night, remember?"

His mother frowned and furrowed her brows. "You know, you're right! I do remember," she said, as she sat up in bed. "It was part of a very peculiar dream. I was being kidnapped so I rang my bell . . ."

". . . and two guys came to rescue you, but we couldn't save you right away . . ."

"They chased after me in a streetcar, I think . . ."

"We chased you in your race car, too."

"But, how do *you* know?"

"Everyone does," Matthew said. "It was broadcast live to the Dreaming Channel. The whole world was watching, Mom."

Matthew's mother didn't quite understand, so he tried to explain as they went down to breakfast. When he was through, she still wasn't sure.

"Was it a dream, or was it real?" she asked Matthew.

"Neither, Mom, we were acting, see? All of us were. It was part of the movie. I won a special Harry Award! But actually, as you and I know, I owe it all to you. So I want you to have it instead of me."

Matthew proudly gave her the Harry. His mother seemed pleased to receive it. Matthew knew it would certainly be an excellent photo opportunity. His mother agreed.

"Go get the camera, dear. I'm almost ready for my close-up, now. But if I'm going to look my best, I'll need hot cup of coffee first."